Simon & Louise

First English edition, 2019 by Conundrum Press

Originally published in French by Sarbacane as two volumes:
520 kms
Un été en apnée

Translation by Aleshia Jensen
Production assistance by Noah van Nostrand
Printed in China by Imago

Library and Archives Canada Cataloguing in Publication
Radiguès, Max de, 1982-
[Simon & Louise. English]
Simon & Louise / Max de Radiguès ; translation by Aleshia Jensen.
Translation of: Simon & Louise.
ISBN 978-1-77262-035-1 (softcover)
1. Graphic novels. I. Jensen, Aleshia, translator II. Title. III. Title: Simon & Louise. English. IV. Title: Simon and Louise.
PN6790.B43R3313 2019 741.5'9493 C2018-905609-6

By the same author:
Moose ISBN 978-1-894994-93-4
Weegee: Serial Photographer (with Wauter Mannaert)
ISBN 978-1-77262-023-8

Conundrum International
Wolfville, Nova Scotia, Canada
www.conundrumpress.com

Conundrum Press acknowledges the financial assistance of the Canada Council for the Arts, the Government of Canada, and the Nova Scotia Creative Industries Fund toward this publication.

Canada Council for the Arts
Conseil des Arts du Canada

Max de Radiguès

DRIIIIIIIIIIIIIIIIING
Class dismissed. Have a great summer...
ZIIIIIIIIIP
Don't forget everything you've learned this year...
See You Next Year!
SIMON!

Heh.
All done!
Summer at last!
Two months in Montpellier for me. Two months without you.
My mom finally let me get a phone.
We'll be able to call each other, text and send pictures every day.
CLICK
Promise?
Promise!
it'll go fast...
TOOOT TOOOT
That's my dad.
i'll miss you!
Same here.
Talk to you tonight!
it'll be fine!
Eeesh
Two months.
That's a long time...

Simon

Search
News Feed
profile
Share: Status Photo Link
"What's on your mind?"
Louise G. is single
15 minutes ago
4 people like this
WHAT ?!
c'mon
c'mon
c'mon
Hello?
TAP TAP TAP
Louise, it's me. What's with your Facebook status?
It's a mistake, right?
I was going to call you. My dad saw our texts. He says I'm too young to be in love.
He doesn't want me to see you anymore. So I don't really have any choice. But we can still be friends, okay? I'll see you in September...
Bye.
Simon, come outside. We didn't go on vacation so you could stay indoors the whole time!
Share: Status Photo Link
"What's on your mind?"
Louise G. is single
19 minutes ago
Deborah and 5 others like this
Deborah: Single for the summer? All those hotties on the beach are all yours!
Louise G. LOL!!! ;-)

Hi, it's Louise, leave a message! BEEP.
TAP
TAP

Hey Louise, it's me. You haven't answered my calls or emails.
Just wanted to hear your voice...
I miss you.
Call me back.
BZZZTT
VRRRR
18:21
Message from:
Louise
Plz dnt call.
Wish I cld talk but can't bc of my dad.
Sorry xx

You okay, Simon? You've been quiet all evening. And you've barely touched your food.
mm-hm, yeah.
Mom?
Yeah?
Umm
Do you think i'm too young to be in love?
Aw you're so cute.
C'mon Mom, i'm serious!
You're so annoying! Just forget it.
When i met your dad, i was five years older than you. i know we're not together anymore but...
i really loved him.

Love just happens. There's no right age.
Um, speaking of which, you know the guy we met at minigolf, Henry?
The one with the little girl?
Yeah. Well he asked me out for a drink tonight and i was wondering...
Yeah of course, Mom. You should go.
Thanks, i'll get going then... i won't be too late... He's probably a moron like all the others...
Don't worry about the dishes.
Heh heh!
23:03
New message to: Louise
Your dad can't keep us apart. i won't let him!

BEEP BEEP BEEP
BRRRRR
Come on.
Shhh... Stay here, boy.
GNNNN GNN
Hi Mom,
Cedric called last night and invited me sailing with his family. We're sleeping on the boat. Not sure if i'll have reception.
Love ya xxx
Simon
PS: Was Henry a moron?

MONTPELLIER
I can take you as far as the exit for Bordeaux.
That's perfect!
You're a bit young to be travelling alone, aren't you?
I'm going to see my girlfriend. My mom was supposed to bring me but something came up.
Thanks again!
You're right at the start of the A62 so getting a ride should be a breeze. Good luck!
Heh, heh. Already made it pretty far and it's only 8:30 a.m. Just a few hours till I see you, Louise!
MONTPELLIER
I'll prove to your dad that it's meant to be.
MONTPELLIER

MONTPELLIER
MONTPELLIER
HEY!
Uh... Hey.
What do you think you're doing?
Uh...
i've been trying to hitch a ride for over an hour! And you?!
You come over and stand just up the road from me?!
Think you can jump the line just 'cuz you're some snotty little rich kid?
With your little sigggnnn...
No...i...i...i didn't...

it's just that...
it's just that what?!
Don't think i can get a ride, that it?
TAP TAP
Stop it!!!
Ss... sorry.
i...
i wasn't trying to cut in line. i've never hitchhiked before...
...i need to get to Montpellier and be back in Arcachon tomorrow night...
Or else my mom will...
You running away? That it?
Haha! First time running away i bet! Right?

MONTPELLIER
TA-DAA!
MONTPELLIER
BRRR
Want a sandwich? Ham 'n' cheese or corned beef?
Liver!
Mmmh Thanks, haven't eaten since last night.
So you do this a lot?
What do you mean?
Always on the road...
Ha, ha! No.
My parents think I'm with a friend in Nice.
You want to be free though? Because you're a punk?
Free? I guess I just like meeting different people every day and making up whatever story I want.
For one month a year, I can forget about family, school and friends. And just think about me, meet people who judge me on who I am, not what I do.

I go by the name of Jack London when I'm on the road.
And your bag's White Fang?
Haha
I'm Sim...
BEEEEP
Don't want to separate you two but we've only got one spot in the back.
MONTPELLIER
I know you're in a hurry... but do you mind if...
Go for it.
Thanks! Good luck on the road!
TAP TAP
You need a hitching name.
RRRRRRRRRR
How about Martin Eden. That's "my" best novel.
BYE!
I have a hitching name!

MONTPELLIER
MONTPELLIER
Already 11:30 ugh. Shit, this is taking forever.
Hey!
Where you headed?
Um...
Montpellier.

Same. Hop in!
Really?
Cool!
Thanks!
Thanks a bunch!
You been waiting a while?
Sorta.
Clement.
Uh, Martin.
Nice to meet you.
You can throw your bag in the back if you like.
So, what's a kid like you doing on the side of a highway?

My mom was supposed to bring me to see my girlfriend.
You ran away, that it?
Uh...no...i...
Ha! Don't worry! It was just a question.
No sweat if you don't feel like talking.
i remember running away when i was about your age.
i snuck out my window in the middle of the night and walked for hours!
i was cold and hungry. i got home just before my mom came into my room to wake me up.
My parents never even noticed.
Ha, ha!
i told my mom i was going sailing with a friend and that i'd be back tomorrow.
Ha! Aren't you sly!

Wait, why are we off the highway?

Ah, you're awake! Sleep well?
Um where are we?
Just south of Carcassonne.
But Montpellier isn't south of Carcassonne.
Are are you not going to Montpellier anymore?
Mister Clement?
Just need to make a quick stop first. Won't take long.
i'll drop you in Montpellier after.
ah
i'm actually kind of in a hurry. i'll get out here.

Huh?! Don't be an idiot Martin, we're in the middle of nowhere.
i told you, i'll drop you right after!!!
That's really nice of you but i'd rather get out here.
Are you kidding me?!
Wait?! You don't think that... Shit!
i have a son for crying out loud!
Listen, i'm sorry, i shouldn't have lost my temper.
PAM

YOU LITTLE SHIT!
I...
Get out of my car.
GET OUT OF MY CAR!
I have to come back this way. You'd be wise to steer clear so I don't run into you!
Shit, my bag...

Shit! My phone is in my bag!
What was i thinking?
i'm in the middle of nowhere.
Nobody knows i'm here...

Calm down
Calm down
Calm down
Calm down
Right... I won't walk in his direction in any case.
I can't be too far from the next town.

I wonder if he really has a son.
Shit!
Am I just paranoid?
No.
Yes?
Ha, ha!
I really got him good!

That's the first time I ever punched someone.
Heh heh.

Man it's hot!
i'm thirsty.
i wonder how long i've been walking.
20 minutes? 1 hour? 2?
i wonder where i am.
Maybe i'm super close to Montpellier.
Maybe i can even walk the rest of the way and not have to hitchhike.
BRRRRR
BRRRRRRRR
BRRRRRRRRRRRR

Phew, wasn't him.
I should maybe stay off the road.
What's that sound?
Water?

Cool!
WHOA!
So cold!

Is it safe to drink?
Getting the shits right now is all I need.
Well, I don't have much choice...
PFFRRR
BLARGH
BL...BL...BLL
What am I even doing here?

So, i'm in the middle of nowhere and i've got...
...4 euros 60 and two sticks of gum.
Aahh.
Okay.
i can't stay here...
...waiting for something to happen.
WATCH OUT!

Catch that sheep!
Sheep?
He's headed right for you! Catch him!
How exactly am i supposed to catch it?
Hey sheep!
Shit...
No, this way!

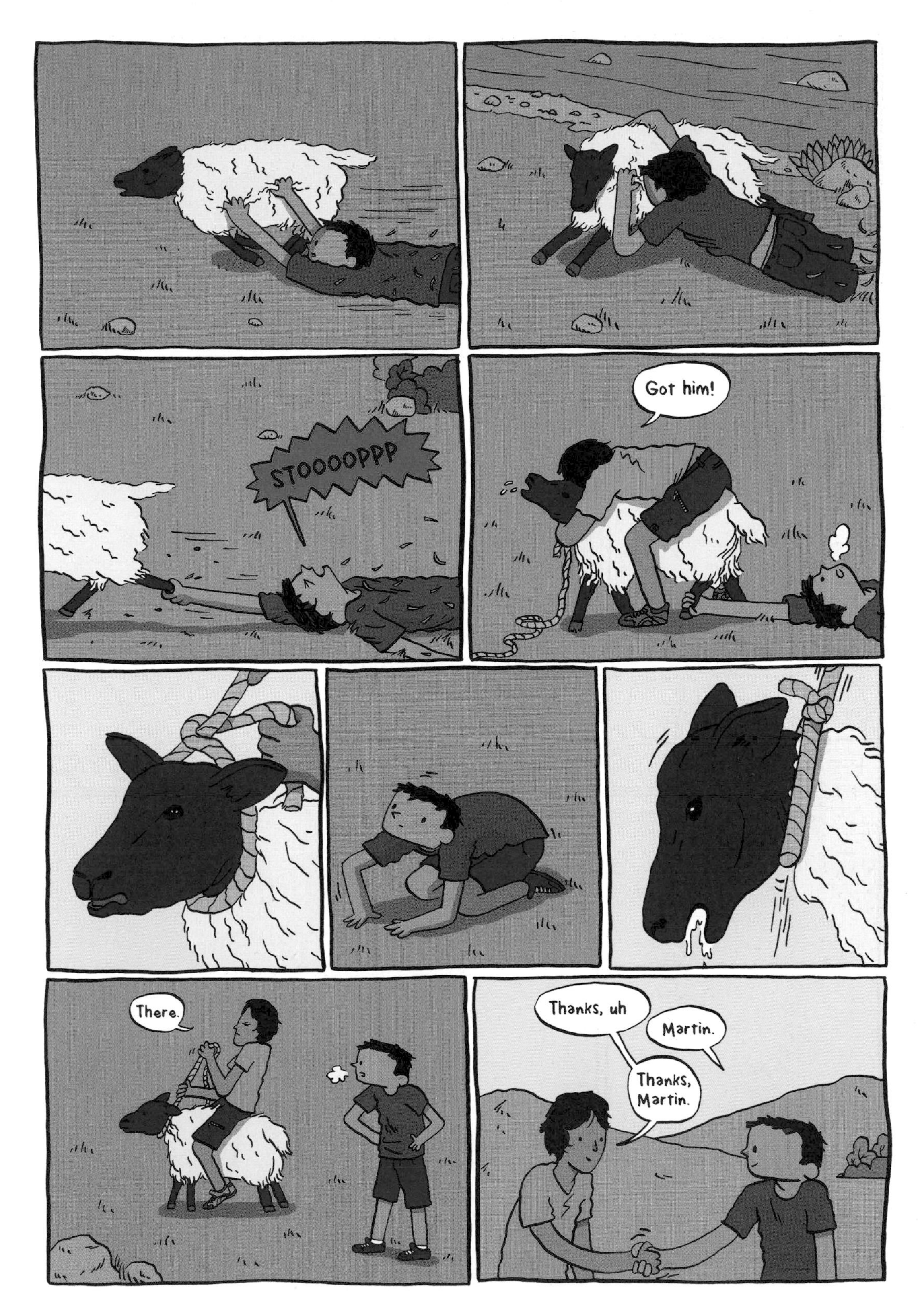
STOOOOPPP
Got him!
There.
Thanks, uh
Martin.
Thanks, Martin.

i'm Alex.
This your sheep?
Yeah.
Does he have a name?
Of course not. We don't name animals we eat.
You're going to eat him???
Yeah, we're killing him tonight to eat him tomorrow.
i don't even want to think about how mad my dad would've been if i'd lost him.
"HiS GREAT TRADiTiON"
You coming?
What's this great tradition?
My dad was a nomad.
?
Like a gypsy.
He went sedentary when he met my mom.

But every year he hits the road for a month...
And I've been going with him ever since I was five...
My mom hates camping though. She joins us on the last night....
Come onnnnnnn...
This sheep's a real ass!
Haha! Want to sit?
You could bring your parents and come eat with us.
We always invite tons of people. One sheep for two people is way too much...
Did I say something wrong?
I'm not from here.
I...I ran away.
Whoa! Spill!
Well, there's this girl...

Haha! I can't believe you punched him in the face while he was driving!
HA, HA!

Anyway, i'm sure my dad won't mind if you stay with us tonight...
Cool...
He might even be able to drop you in Montpellier. it's super close...
Really?!
And you can help us kill the sheep...
...
Kill the sheep...
Come on, let's go.
OK.
Kill the sheep...
Shit, where'd the sheep go?
THERE!
Ha, ha
Hurry!
There he goes!

Here we are.
Whoa...
Ahh you're back.
So how did the last walk of the condemned go?
Totally fine.
And you even brought back company.
Martin. Nice to meet you, sir.
No sirs here. Call me Anton.
Uh Dad, Martin was headed to Montpellier but he ran into a bit of trouble on the way.
Can he stay with us tonight?
Sure! Do you want to use my phone to let your parents know?
Uh, no, it's okay. I already called my mom.
Perfect. You can help us with the sheep.
You're really going to kill it?
Well we're not going to eat it alive!
Ha, ha no.

I'll go get some drinks. You must be parched.
Yes! Thanks.
Aaaah. It's so cool here!
Yeah, we always finish our holiday here. The farmer lets us stay and we buy him a sheep in exchange.
That's AWESOME!
Mm. Still, I wouldn't mind having a "normal" vacation at the beach like you at some point.
Yeah... well... it's not really that great when you're by yourself.
Snack is served, dear sirs!
JAFFA
Tomorrow it'll be spit-roasted lamb. We always invite everyone in the neighbourhood.
It cooks for the whole day, so we'll kill it tonight.

Martin, since it's your first time, i'll explain how it works.
First we cut his throat. He keeps moving for a while but don't worry, it's a natural nervous system reaction.
We cut off the hooves and make incisions here and there so we can cut him up more easily.
Then we remove the organs and hang the sheep upside down to drain all the blood out properly.
That's all you need to know for tonight. Questions?
Um...
My dad's acting like this is totally normal but you can wait here if you want.
Umm, no... no i'll come.
Well, gentlemen! Let's go fetch the condemned.
Sometimes i get this weird feeling this is his favourite part of our vacation.

You sure you're all right? You really don't have to.
It's the same deal every summer but it still churns my stomach a bit...
I'll be OK. Don't worry about me.
Here we go then.
Good evening, sirs!
We'll lie him down on the tarp.
Hold his feet firmly together.
Ready?
Yes...

BLECH

Brrrrrrr
You OK?
Better, yeah.
Want to eat something?
You'll feel better.
mm
Want a hot dog or are you vegetarian now?
I could go for a hot dog!

Heh, heh
Doo doo doot
Ha, ha
You have to stick it near the flame but not directly in it.
Must be ready, no?
Right, all done. Don't have much of an appetite now. I'm going to clean up and head to bed.
Ok Dad.
Martin, I'll bring you to Montpellier tomorrow first thing. That work for you?
Thanks Mister Anton.
Nice night. You can sleep outside.
Quit it! My hair.
Goodnight.

My dad would've liked you to stay tomorrow.
I told him that you really needed to go.
I would've liked you to stay too.
So what are you going to say when you find her?
Who?
Louise of course! Your girlfriend.
Oh! Yeah
right.
I dunno. Haven't really thought about it, actually.
Ha!
Haha
What?!
You've come all this way and you don't even know what you're going to say.
Haha!
Haha.

Goodnight. Thanks. Not sure what I would've done without you.
You're welcome. It was nice to have some company other than my dad.
What am I going to say to her?
Will she think I'm romantic or just crazy?
I should've let her dumb dad decide for us.
I'll find her and kiss her, and she'll understand.
Yeah, that's what I'll do.
Hop to, boys!

Do you drink coffee, Martin?
Um, i'll try some, sure.
LAIT
Yuk!
All set, Martin?
Mm.
Bye.
Thanks for everything.
We'll be here next year, same time! Come say hi!
Bye!

Montpellier-Est
FREJORGUES
NIMES
MARSEILLE
LYON
Okay if I drop you at the station?
Yeah that's perfect.
it's really too bad you couldn't stay for dinner.
You earned it.
Mm.

Thank you, sir.
Anton, Martin. Anton.
Thanks, Anton.
Right. Should I call her now?
Is it classier if I just run into her on the street?
I know where she hangs out during the day. I can probably find her.
Or worst case I can just call her.
EXPOSITI
BUL
INFORMATIO
Looks like everything's in the same neighbourhood.
Hey Louise...
Haha, yeah it's me! I ran away and crossed the country for you.
Yeah, yeah. It was dangerous but I won't let anything come between us.
I would've travelled across the world for you.

Can't wait to see her expression...
Simon? No I go by Martin now.
Oh! You mean what am I doing here? I ran away to find you...
Louise.
ARCADE ZONE
Louise...
Huh. Where can she be?
MARTIN

Hey Jack.
Heyyy Martin! I thought it was you!
Glad to see you made it too.
How'd it go?
Well...
Pretty smoothly. I got here this morning.
Oh, shit.
We're heading down to Barcelona tonight if you want to run away for a bit longer.
That's nice of you, but I have to go.
Bye Jack.
Bye Martin.
See you, everyone!
See ya Martin
Bye!
See ya.
Catch you on the road!

HOBO GOSS
Already?! Maybe I should just call...
A phone booth... A phone booth...
Alfred
You can never find one when you actually need one!
Aha!
Of course.
Seriously?

I ♥ TONTON
It works!
Hey!
Haha!
Heeyyy!
Hey!
Yoo-hoo!
Louise!
LOUISE!
L..
huh?

Hey!
i missed you...
Since yesterday?
Yeah...
Me too, babe.
BABE?! Who is this guy? Who does he think he is?

BLACK BIRD
It had nothing to do with her dad.
THUMP
CLANG
CLANG
CLANG
CLANG
CLANG
CLANG
KLUNK
CLING
Ti
Ti
Ti
DOOO DOOO
DOO DOOO
DOO DOOO

Hi Mom?
No, i'm in Montpellier.
Yeah Montpellier.
Yeah.
No, i'm okay. Don't worry.
Can you come pick me up?
i'll explain later. No Mom
Don't get mad.
i know.
See you at the train station at 7?
mhm. 7:30.
Thanks.
Love you too, Mom.
Bye. And sorry.
Mom?
Do you like mutton?

Louise

Are you sure you want to change your status from in a relationship to single?
CONFIRM
CANCEL
Confirmed!
No!
Stop!
Too late... You're single now, honey...
GRRRR
Pinch
Pinch
Not cool. I told you not to do that!
Heh...
Oh! You already got one like!
And it's a guy too!
Do you know an Antoine VDH?
He's in my class...
Woohoo... an admirer.
Deborah commented: "Those hotties on the beach are all yours!"
She did?
See? Deborah agrees! You should enjoy your vacation and all the...
Do what you want. I don't care!
Heh heh
LOL!!!
BBZZTT... BBBZZZTTT...
Ahh! It's him! It's Simon!

Don't answer!
Too late...
Hello?
Hi?
Louise, it's me. What's with your Facebook status?
It's a mistake, right?
I was going to call you...
Umm...
That's a movie for big kids.
But dad! It's Spiderman!
My dad saw our texts. He says I'm too young to be in love...
He doesn't want me to see you anymore. So I don't really have any choice. But we can still be friends, okay?
I'll see you in September...
Bye.

Why didn't you say something?
You could've said it was me...
Leave me alone!
GIRLS? WE'RE GOING TO THE MARKET, YOU COMING?
But...
I...
Manon's coming! I'm staying here! See you later...
BBZZZTT...
Hey Louise, it's me. You haven't answered my calls or emails. Just wanted to hear your voice...
I miss you.
BBZZZTT...
Plz dnt call. Wish I cld talk but can't bc of my dad.
Sorry xx

But how can you say that, you sound like a conservative!
Just because you're on the left doesn't mean you need to sit on the sidelines.
Just a splash dear...
Haha!
Mom? Can we be excused?
Yes. You know how they are once they get going. i won't make you suffer through it.
But what's app
How come my dad always has to talk about politics and money when he's had a couple drinks?
Well, he's going to get along great with mom's boyfriend.
How are things with him?
David? i don't want to like him, but he's actually really nice to me.
And he's really awesome with my mom.
Yeah, he seems cool.
SHHH
Louise?
Mm?

I'm sorry about earlier with Simon...
It's fine. I'm over it.
What do you mean?
You guys are back together?
No, but I've been thinking...
Simon was cute and super nice. I think he might even be in love with me...
It's cool to have someone in love with you...
But...
Do I love him? Or just like him?
Pfft I don't even know if I know the difference...
I don't know if I've ever really been in love, like for real...
Like, not the way your mom and David are in love, you know?
Mm.
So, you're single, cuz?
Yep.
Sweet! Those beach hotties are all ours!
CLAP CLAP
Ha! You're crazy...

KFFF
KWSH
KFFF
Toc
poc
Oops... Sorry, I...
I...

S...Sorry.
All good!
Quentin.
Louise.
HEY! You playing or what?
See you around, Louise.
THUMP

Oh my god it was so embarrassing!
Haha! I wish I'd been there!
Pffft...
Which one is he?
Mm
Ah! Those two over there, looking at something on their phone. The one with the hair...
Ooooo! You didn't tell me he was XH!
XH?
Extra hot.
And his friend too!!!
You think?
They're okay I guess, but they seem kinda d...
dumb.
DOPE!
They seem super cool!
Pack up your things, girls! We're leaving.

Are you girls ready to go?
Let me carry something!
Mm
Not quite... You go ahead and we'll meet you in the parking lot in a sec...
All set, cuz?
All set!
Um Manon, the car is the other way.
We're taking the scenic route.
Where are we going?
Oh!
Manon!
No!
Hey guys!
Manon!
'Sup
Hey...
Do we know you?

Hey, you in the back, you're the girl who was snorkelling, aren't you?
Louise, right?
Um, yes.
Yeah, and I'm her cousin, Manon.
Hey Manon. I'm Luca.
Want to join us?
mm
Yes, sit.
Actually we have to get back to Montpellier.
Cool! We're from Montpellier too.
Are you coming back tomorrow?
There's a movie playing outside tonight at this square ummm...
Oh yeah, I know the spot.
Maybe we'll see you there?
Definitely see you there!!!
Bye
See you later then...
Bye girls!
See you!
Bye Louise!
You're crazy!
Pff they're the crazy ones. Crazy about us!
Haha!
I feel like you'll be forgetting Simon in no time...

TA-DAA
So?
WOWW!
Straight out of a music video!
What about you?
Uhh... I was going to wear this...
WHY ME?
A Snoopy T-shirt and shorts?
It's a cool shirt, no?
She actually thinks it's cool!
And the shorts?
They're just shorts. I wear them all the time.
LOUISE! You look like an eight-year-old boy!
How on earth did you ever get Simon to fall for you?
Lucky for you that I'm here!
I got you covered.
Haha! It's like I'm on reality TV!
Manon Fashion!
I dunno ...
Hehe!

Umm no.
No?! Okay.
BITCH
So?
Is this a joke?!
Haha! Yeah!
Uhh
Argh
Maybe I should just wear my own stuff? 'Cause this...
Mm ok.
This is perfect, no?
Mm yeah. With your hair up though.
Haha! I used to dream of being Ferris Bueller!
I bet. You're totally a Ferris.
Heh, heh
It's kinda weird that your mom's pregnant.
I think it's kinda cool.
I'm going to have a little brother!
Yeah it's still weird. They're too old to have a baby.
You better get used to the idea, seeing as your mom is so into David. You might be a big sister soon too...
What?!
You're joking...
Right?
You haven't noticed how our moms have only talked about babies all summer?
No!
So what?!
Oh... shit...
NO!
Come on, keep it together. We've got somewhere to be.
Mm

Over here, girls! We saved you a spot!
Mom, we're going to sit closer to the front.
Ok see you after the movie.
Yep.
Manon, i'm serious! Right after the credits.
Ugh! Okaaay. Geez.
Hmph
You okay?
Come on, let's go.
Maybe if she got pregnant she'd stop treating me like a baby.

You see them?
Mm
If they stood us up I'm going to lose it!
There they are!!!
Huh?
Where?!
Excuse me.
Sorry.
Excuse me.
Oops.
Excuse me.
Hey!
Hmph.
Argh
Hey.
Hello...
Hey.
kiss
kiss
Have a seat!
I didn't think you'd show.
Same.

Arthur! Go get us some drinks and snacks.
What? But i'm watching the movie.
God! Come on! Just do it.
Okay fine. What do you guys want?
Um, i guess i'll ha...
Four cokes n' four hot dogs!
Do you have some cash?
What?!
Wow, what a gentleman! Can't even buy the girls a couple of cokes!
Okayy
Wait, Arthur. i've got some money.
No don't! His dad won the lottery.
Here, for mine and Manon's at least.
Thanks.
And i'd actually like an Orangina and some candy. And Manon drinks diet coke.
Ok.
Cheap.
Ketchup and mustard on the hot dogs!

Psst Manon. You see that?
Totally not cool, hey?
Manon?
Ma...
Ah right... Ok what...
Crap. What have i gotten myself into?
Sup?
is he going to kiss me?
He's cute, but i don't even know him.
Whatever. it's summer! And if Manon is doing it...
He doesn't kiss anything like Simon...
Oh Simon. What am i even doing?
Oh! Arthur's back. i'll help him with the drinks!
Stay... He's fine...
Wait, let me help you.
Thanks Louise.
No, thank you.

Do you want mine Luca?
Mm!
You didn't get anything, Arthur?
No, I'm not hungry.
Wanna head out?
Myeahm!
Yeah!
What? No! We have to stay. We said we'd meet our parents after the movie.
Relax cuz.
Don't worry, there's like 45 minutes left.
We'll be back in time, I promise.
Umm okay.
Pss-psst
Ha, ha shut up!
Aren't you coming Arthur?
No thanks. I'm going to stay and finish the movie.

Where are we going?
You'll see.
We can't be late though...
Here we are!

A tree?
You don't expect us to climb that thing do you?!
YEAH!
I mean maybe I could, but Manon?
HEY!
TAP
But yeah you're right.
Heh, heh!
Ha, ha!
Hey boys! Did you hear us?!
Ah.
KLKLKLUMK
You got the ladder?
Yeah, don't worry.

So?
Woww! You made a city treehouse.
Huh?
That's high!
No, no. Wasn't us who built it.
Yeah, we're a bit old to be building treehouses.
Last year there were cabins like this all over the city.
People slept in them. It was to protest about the crisis or...
Wasn't it those Namonymous guys or whatever?
With those, like, masks?
Anyway, they're gone but the treehouses are still here.
So we kinda took this one over.
That's cool.

Here we go again...
You're really pretty Louise.
Stop.
Stop!

God! What part of stop don't you understand?!
What's going on?
What's going on is we're leaving!
Wait!
What the hell did you do, Quentin?
Yeah! What did you do to my cousin, Pony-face?!
N...nothing...
Nothing bad.
Manon, let's go!
Wait...
I'm sorry I...
Hands off!
SMACK
...
AH!
LOUISE!
AAAAAAA

LOUISE!
Louise?
i'm
i'm okay.
Humph.
Manon! C'mon. We're leaving.

If you set one foot near her I'll scratch your eyes out!
But
That clear?!
Louise...
See you tomorrow, gorgeous.
See you tomorrow! Sorry about all this.
You okay?
BOOHOOHOO
Hey, calm down. It's all right. You're in one piece. It's over.
BOOHO
I thought I was going to die!
Me too. Don't ever scare me like that again.
TAP
TAP
Come on, let's go.

Louise?
mm-hm.
Quentin, he...
Did he push you?
What? No, no. He didn't. My foot got stuck in the ladder and...
Oof!
I really got scared for a minute. I thought he pushed you.
No, no
So I guess maybe I shouldn't have threatened to scratch his eyes out!
You said that?!
Ha, ha!
He, he
And you called him Pony-face.
HA HA HA HA HA HA HA HA HA HA HA HA HA HA HA HA HA HA HA HA
Pony-face
Haha!
It really suits him.
Perfectly! Ha, ha!
He's actually kinda cute.
I mean, so are ponies.
Not sure you would kiss a pony though.
A dolphin maybe but not a pony.
Ha, ha!

Louise?
Mm-hm.
Why did you get so upset?
It's Quentin. He... He wouldn't stop groping me.
That's it?
Well...
I told him to stop a bunch of times but...
He was like a slobbering dog...
BAAAH
Ha, ha!
It doesn't bug you? To have someone feel you up like that?
Meh, you know me, I don't really have that problem.
Luca spent the whole evening fondling my socks and didn't even notice!
You stuffed your bra with socks?!
We're not all lucky enough to have boobs.
Ha, ha! You're nuts Manon!
He, he!
Where are we anyway? We should be there by now.
I was following you.

We didn't come this way before...
DANGER
Come on, we must have turned the wrong way.
Raaah. We're so in for it!
BRRRRRR
Hey ladies! Need a ride?
Hey! I'm talking to you!
OH!
Shit, you deaf?!

DUMB SLUTS!
Louise...
I want to go home.
We're almost there...
I'm scared Louise...
Don't be. I'm scared too but don't be.
We got this.

Wasn't it that way?!
You think?
Around the corner, no?
You sure? That way?
Louise!
Wait.
BAM
mf.
LOUISE!
You ok?
Oww
Sorr...
AAAAAHHH
GET UP!
COME ON!
AAAH

You okay sweetie? My bad, I wasn't looking where I was going.
...
I didn't mean to scare you, sorry.
Ehm
Isn't it a bit late to be wandering the streets by yourselves?
We're lost.
Hey shhhh.
We can't stay out here all night.
Mm.
We're looking for this place with an outdoor movie thing? Our parents are waiting for us.
Ah! You're pretty close but the movie must've finished ages ago.
Come on. I'll be your guide.
Are you sure we can trust him?
I think so.
HA, HA!
What's so funny?!
I've been babysitting all day. You're the second bunch of kids I've helped out.
This morning I saw this kid hitching to Montpellier. His girlfriend broke up with him and he was going to win her back...
What was his name?!

Uhh...
Martin.
Oh.
How come?
Oh, no reason. Just curious.
Right, it's over there. I'll leave you here.
I'm not sure your parents would be super thrilled to see you roll up late and with a punk.
Thanks
Bye!
Everyone's gone.
Almost.
Shit.
Yeah, what you said.

Uh
We
Yes?
We just went for a little walk.
We meant to be back on time...
But...
But we got lost! We kept going in circles.
Yeah!
Girls...
Do you know what this is?
A cellphone?
We're paying for these super expensive things in case there's ever a problem...
And the first time there is a problem, we can't reach either of you!
I left mine at home.
Louise, I called you at least fifty times!
It was on silent...
I..I.. didn't think to...
Come on, we'll figure all this out at home.
Okay?
Shall we?
Okay.

Manon?
You asleep?
No.
Me neither.
CLICK
No don't!
We'll get in even more trouble.
True, we've been punished enough for one night.
I can't believe we have to clean the entire house tomorrow.
Bah, I feel like we got off pretty easy.
It should only take a couple hours with both of us.
Ughh. But I was supposed to see Luca tomorrow.
Yeah?

Yeah, he's so sweet. We've got so much in common...
Like our iPods are 80% the same music! Isn't that rad?
And he wants to be an oceanographer! To look after whales! That's seriously been my favourite animal since I was six.
Wasn't it unicorns?
Whales have always been my favourite non-imaginary animal.
You guys talked about all that?
Yeah, and lots of other stuff.
I didn't talk about anything with Quentin.
There were just weird long silences where I tried not to let him get too close...
You guys are just a bit shy. It'll go better next time.
I don't think I want there to be a next time.
What?!
Wait, you can't ditch him! I really like Luca! You need to come too.
So there's four of us.
You made me dump Simon two days ago and now I'm not allowed to be single?!
Make up your mind!
Please Louise. Just don't dump him yet okay?
Good night.

YUK!
Why do I have to do the dishes?
It's so gross!
Because I'm literally cleaning the toilets. Quit complaining.
EWWW!
CLING
SPLATCH
Pweh... ugh... pfft...

Are we almost done?
We still have to vacuum your mom's room and do the bathroom.
Okay, well I think this is good enough. We've been scrubbing all morning while our parents are relaxing on the beach!
We're almost done...
Whatever, I'm done. I'm going to see Luca.
What?! Wait... We'll be done in an hour...
Do what you want but I'm outta here!
We're not maids, y'know.
I'm serious! What's this weird sadistic shit of a punishment?!
It was your mom's idea.
So you coming or not?
Umm
Okay well, call when you want to meet up!
Wait! I made us grilled cheese?
Manon!
WHAK
Ah shit!

Arghh
BAMS
UGHHHHHH
BBBZZZTTT...
Yeah, what?
It's me. Listen, sorry about just now... Seriously.
It's okay.
Come meet us!
I'm still not done.
Who cares! Just come!
Come! Quentin is dying to see you. He's been sulking since I got here.
Really?
You should see his downtrodden little pony-face. It's almost heartbreaking.
Haha! Okay. I'll come, but for you not him!
Where are you?

CLAC
NANCY
TMNT
BASEWOOD
EXPO
Bulu
Hello!

LOUISE!
Hey!
Yoo-hoo!
Hey!
He's alone?
Why is it just him?
Where's Manon?
And here we go...
Did you miss me?
Uh yeah, i missed you.
Since yester-day?
is he stupid or something?
Yeah?
Me too babe.

Babe?! Who does he think he is?!
I bet this is all part of Manon's little scheme!
Where's everyone else?
We'll meet them in the park.
CLANG CLANG CLANG CLANG CLANG
What the?
CLANG CLANG CLANG
Simon?
Oh boy you're really losing it.
You're gonna go nuts if you start imagining Simon everywhere...
Give Pony-face a chance at least.
You cool babe?
Ahhh! Haha!
What?
Nothing... I'm fine. All good.
Come on, let's go find the others.

LOUISE!
So?
Didn't I tell you he was nuts about you?
You're such a little con artist.
Hehe.. I know.
Darling
Haha!
Hi Arthur!
Hi Louise. How're you?
Good. How was the movie?
Move it, Arthur!
SMACK
Don't you ever get sick of being a third wheel?
Seeing everyone make out when you've never even kissed anyone. Must be rough...

How about you go get us some ice cream?
Maybe the fat ice cream dude will give you a big smooch.
HA, HA!
You can always try your luck with his daughter if not...
Yeah. She's like six. She can probably help you out.
You should buy some candy first though, so you don't show up empty-handed!
BAM! HA, HA!
Heh, heh
Manon!
Unless you're more into boys?
Oh man! I was joking but you're totally blushing!!
Ha!
You're into boys?!
HA, HA!
HE, HE!

Leave him alone!
Hey we were just joking around, babe!
Arrr! And don't you "babe" me!
If you call me "babe" one more time you're gonna get it!
Got that, Pony-face?
But but... Louise we're in love.. You...
We're not in love! We don't even know each other. Just because we kissed doesn't mean we're meant to be together!
Babe...
Okay fair warning!
SPLASH
Let's go, Arthur!
We're leaving!
LOUISE!

Pony-face?
Ha, ha
PFRR
I can't believe you pushed him in! He doesn't even get it!
But babe! Babe?!
Ha, ha!
Thanks for doing that for me.
You're welcome.
I did it for me too... I couldn't stand him anymore!
Anyway, it's the last time I go along with one of Manon's dumb plans.
Bah it's not her fault.
Where to now?
I want to show you something...

This your place?
No
it's my dad's boss's place but he's on vacation.
Come...
This way.
i have to water the plants and look after the fish.
The fish?
Ta-daa!
Click
Whoooa!
it's so pretty.
Want to feed them while i water the plants?
A few pinches of this...
Um, okay.
Hehe!

Want to go for a swim?
Where?
There's a pool out back.
This place is a real paradise!
See you later...
i wish i'd brought my bathing suit.
No need. No one's here. We can go in our underwear.
Umm

YAAH!
Jump in!
Umm
i'll turn around.
Don't look okay!
Promise
Come on! it's really warm.
SPLASH
So? Nice, isn't it?
Mm.
FRRR! Hewk, hewk... Wait till i get you!
Ha, ha!

Why do you hang around with Quentin and Luca when they treat you like that?
We were really close friends when we were little. But I haven't really been part of their group for a long time.
Oops
Hehe
Didn't see a thing.
So I'm not really friends with them, but in the summer everyone is out of town and hanging out with them is better than being alone.
I think, anyway.
But since they got girlfriends they've been acting like they're kings of the world.
Yes well, only one of them has a girlfriend now.
Sorry that's kind of my fault.
No it's me not thinking. Two days ago I had a boyfriend I really liked.
What happened?
Manon.
Ah.
Maybe you should call him.
Maybe.
But I don't really know what I want.
I feel a bit lost.
Tell him that.

And you?
Are you with someone?
Umm
Not sure... i don't know.
What do you mean?
Well, i kissed him before he left on vacation.
Before she.
What?
Before she. You said before he left...
Mmmm
No.
OH!
You. You're. Ah! Are you?
NO!
i mean i don't know...
Maybe?
Hey, it's okay.
it's even kind of cool! i've never had a gay friend before!
Um well, i don't know if i...
Well, i've never had a friend who "might be gay or might not be after all."
Hmm.
Thanks...

Louise?
Yeah?
Don't tell anyone okay?
Of course not.
Not even Manon?
Especially not Manon!
Thanks. They already give me a really hard time about not having a girlfriend.
i've got an idea to make you look like a big stud and get rid of Quentin for good.
So we...
Ha, ha! That'll work!
Ok i'm in!
Okay. Turn around. No peeking okay?
Promise.

Hey Manon!
LUCA!
Uh Hi.
Hehe! Hi Arthur!
Hi Louise!
i brought you what you forgot yesterday.
Oh.
Your bra!?!
Oops.
Babe... Louise?!
How did she forget that at yours?
Forgot to put it back on i guess.
TAP TAP

I'm going to swim. Walk me to the water?
Okay
Hehe...
Shhhh, they're right behind us.
Louise...
Who'da thought.
Damn, impressive.
Look at his face!
Your plan worked perfectly!
It's not quite done!
What? But they gobbled up that bra stuff.
That wasn't part of the plan!
Sometimes you've got to improvise!
That way now you've kissed a girl.
That was nice too I...
Ha, ha!
Don't worry. It takes time to know what we want.

KWSI
K
F
F
i'll call Simon
when i get home.

SEEN THIS WIZARD?
KNOCK KNOCK
It's for you.
Thanks.
Hello?
Hi, it's me...
I tried to call your cell a bunch of times but it went straight to voicemail.
Oh, yeah. I lost it.
Already?! How?
It's a long story...
Simon?
I'm sorry about this summer, things were a bit complicated for me.
That's okay.
It was a bit of a complicated summer for me too.

All set for the first day back tomorrow?
Yeah.
You know, i...
i'm looking forward to seeing you.
Same.
See you then...
Yes
Bye.
WIZARD?